EARLY BIRD STORIES

Firefighter Bill & Catch the Crab

Early ★ Reader

First American edition published in 2023 by Lerner Publishing Group, Inc.

An original concept by Elizabeth Dale
Copyright © 2023 Elizabeth Dale

Illustrated by Serena Lombardo

First published by Maverick Arts Publishing Limited

Maverick arts publishing

Licensed Edition
Firefighter Bill & Catch the Crab

For the avoidance of doubt, pursuant to Chapter 4 of the Copyright, Designs and Patents Act of 1988, the proprietor asserts the moral right of the Author to be identified as the author of the Work; and asserts the moral right of the Author to be identified as the illustrator of the Work.

All US rights reserved. No part of this book may be reproduced, stored in a retrieval system, or transmitted in any form or by any means—electronic, mechanical, photocopying, recording, or otherwise—without the prior written permission of Lerner Publishing Group, Inc., except for the inclusion of brief quotations in an acknowledged review.

Lerner Publications Company
An imprint of Lerner Publishing Group, Inc.
241 First Avenue North
Minneapolis, MN 55401 USA

For reading levels and more information, look up this title at www.lernerbooks.com.

Main body text set in Mikado a. Typeface provided by HVD Fonts.

Library of Congress Cataloging-in-Publication Data

Names: Dale, Elizabeth, 1952– author. | Lombardo, Serena, illustrator. | Dale, Elizabeth, 1952– Firefighter Bill. | Dale, Elizabeth, 1952– Catch the crab
Title: Firefighter Bill ; & Catch the crab / Elizabeth Dale ; illustrated by Serena Lombardo.
Other titles: Firefighter Bill (Compilation)
Description: Minneapolis : Lerner Publications, [2023] | Series: Early bird readers. Red (Early bird stories) | "First published by Maverick Arts Publishing Limited." | Audience: Ages 4–8. | Audience: Grades K–1. | Summary: "Firefighter Bill is helping everyone who is stuck. What happens when he gets stuck? Then Jess finds a crab in the sand. She can't catch the crab, who will?"— Provided by publisher.
Identifiers: LCCN 2022020161 (print) | LCCN 2022020162 (ebook) | ISBN 9781728476445 (lib. bdg.) | ISBN 9781728478487 (pbk.) | ISBN 9781728482224 (eb pdf)
Subjects: LCSH: Readers (Primary) | LCGFT: Readers (Publications)
Classification: LCC PE1119.2 .D3443 2023 (print) | LCC PE1119.2 (ebook) | DDC 428.6/2—dc23/eng/20220510

LC record available at https://lccn.loc.gov/2022020161
LC ebook record available at https://lccn.loc.gov/2022020162

Manufactured in the United States of America
1-52225-50665-6/17/2022

Firefighter Bill
&
Catch the Crab

Elizabeth Dale

Illustrated by
Serena Lombardo

Lerner Publications ◆ Minneapolis

The Letter "F"

Trace the lower and upper case letter with a finger. Sound out the letter.

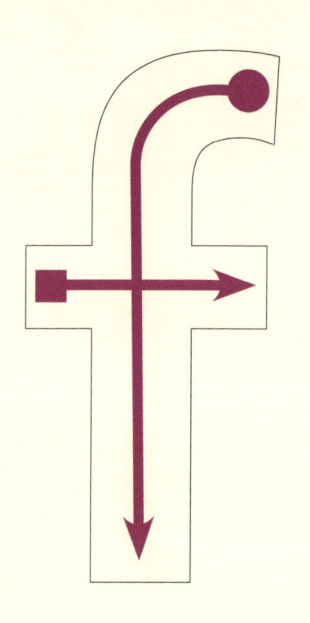

*Around,
down,
lift,
cross*

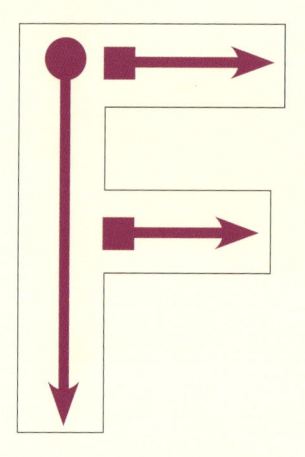

*Down,
lift,
cross,
lift,
cross*

Some words to familiarize:

Bess **Jim** **Meg**

High-frequency words:
is   up   the   in   I

Tips for Reading *Firefighter Bill*

- *Practice the words listed above before reading the story.*
- *If the reader struggles with any of the other words, ask them to look for sounds they know in the word. Encourage them to sound out the words and help them read the words if necessary.*
- *After reading the story, ask the reader why Firefighter Bill needed rescuing.*

Fun Activity

Discuss other things that firefighters do.

Firefighter Bill

Kev is stuck up the tree.
Quick! Call Firefighter Bill.

Firefighter Bill saves Kev. Hooray!

Liz is stuck in the well.
Quick! Call Firefighter Bill.

Firefighter Bill saves Liz. Hooray!

Bess is stuck in the mud.
Quick! Call Firefighter Bill.

Firefighter Bill saves Bess. Hooray!

Firefighter Bill gets stuck in the mud!

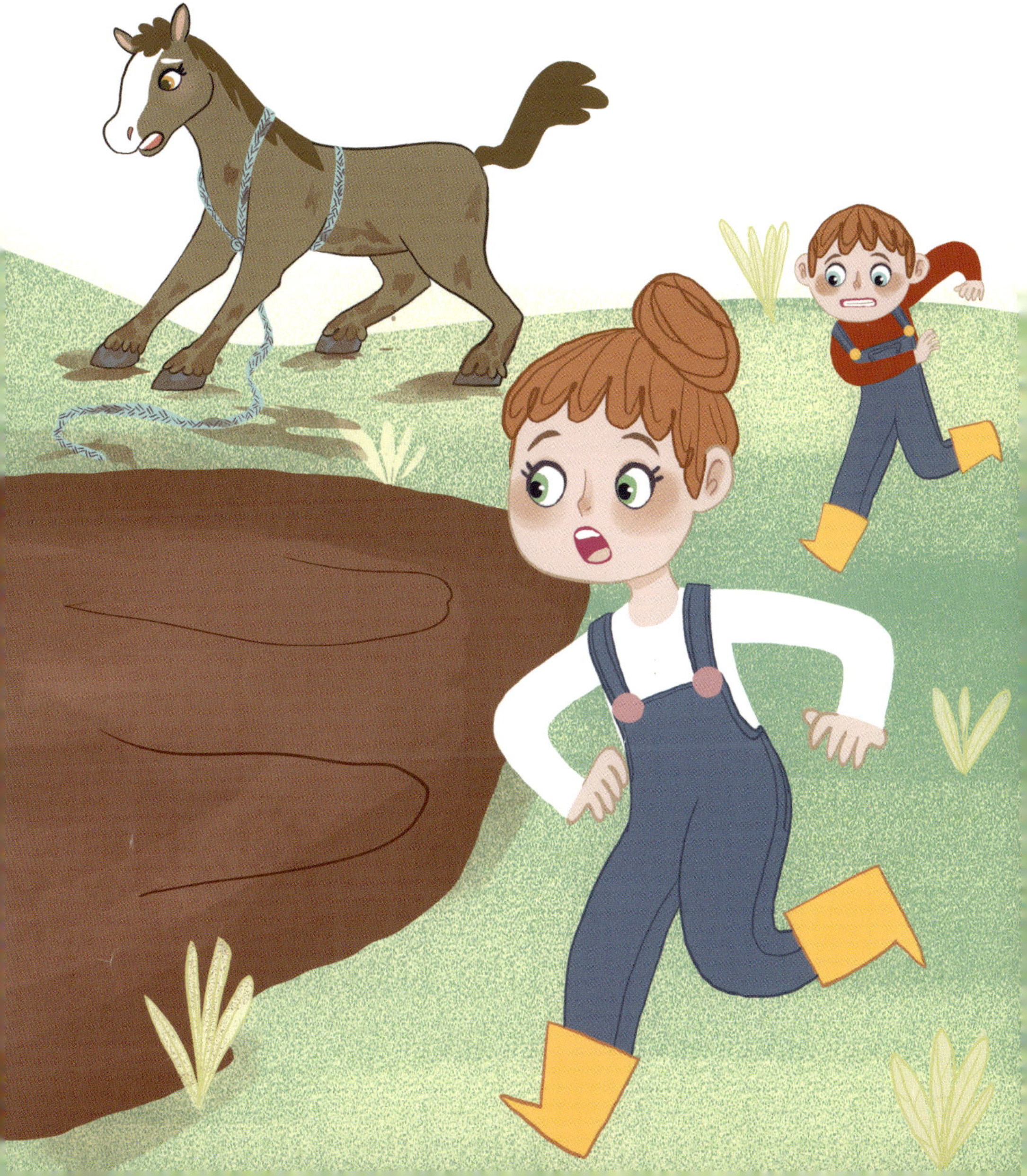

Jim and Meg get stuck in the mud too!

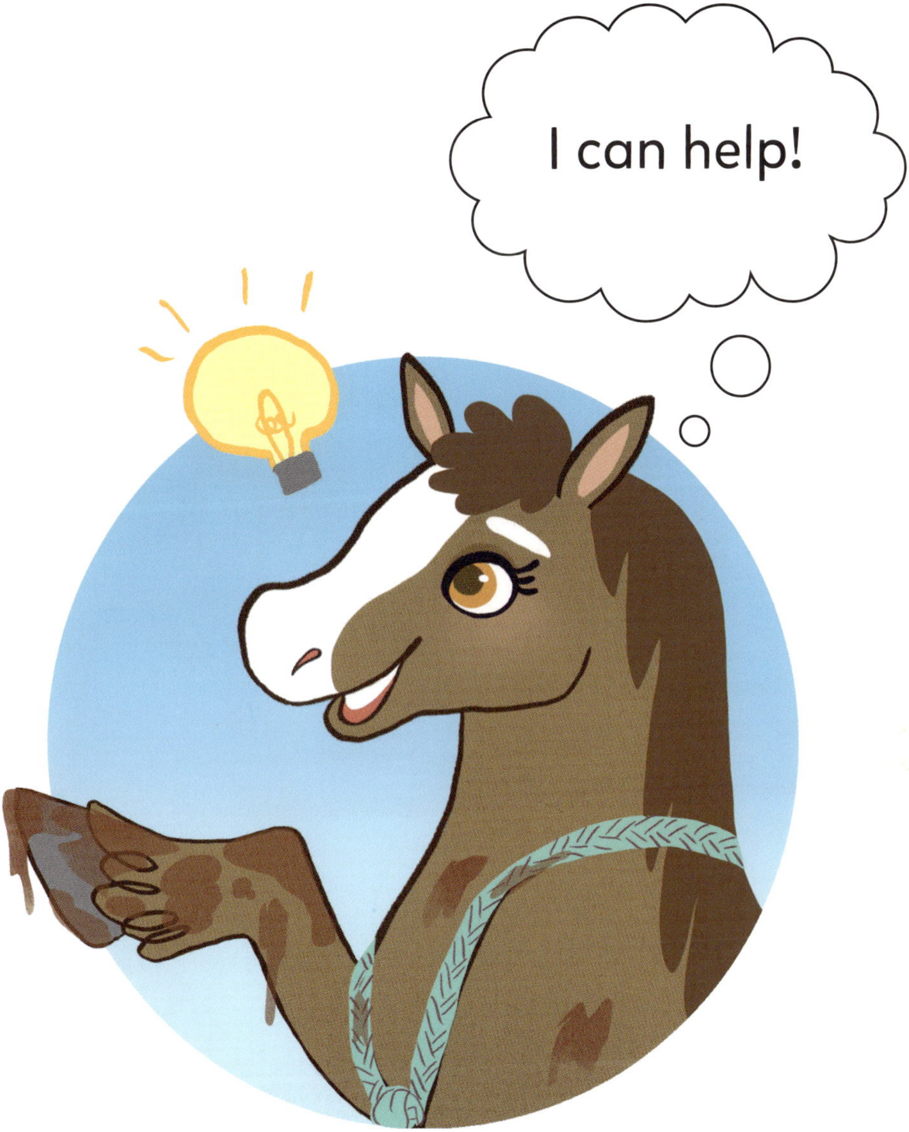
I can help!

Bess saves Firefighter Bill, Jim, and Meg.

Hooray for Bess and Bill!

The Letter "H"

Trace the lower and upper case letter with a finger. Sound out the letter.

Down,
up,
around,
down

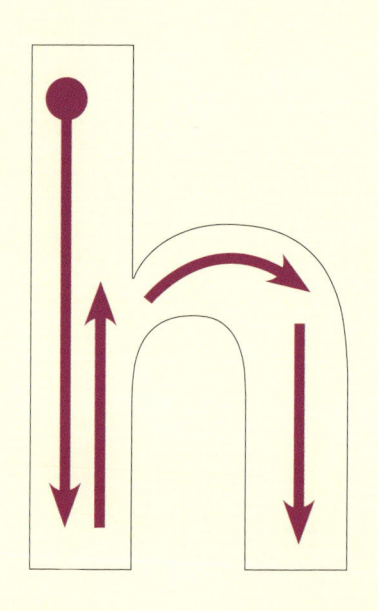

Down,
lift
down,
lift,
cross

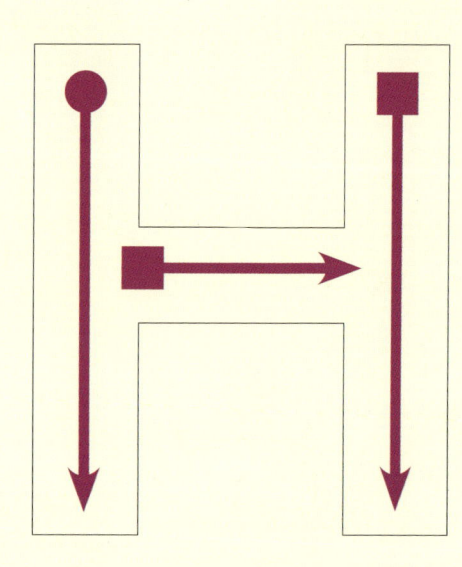

Some words to familiarize:

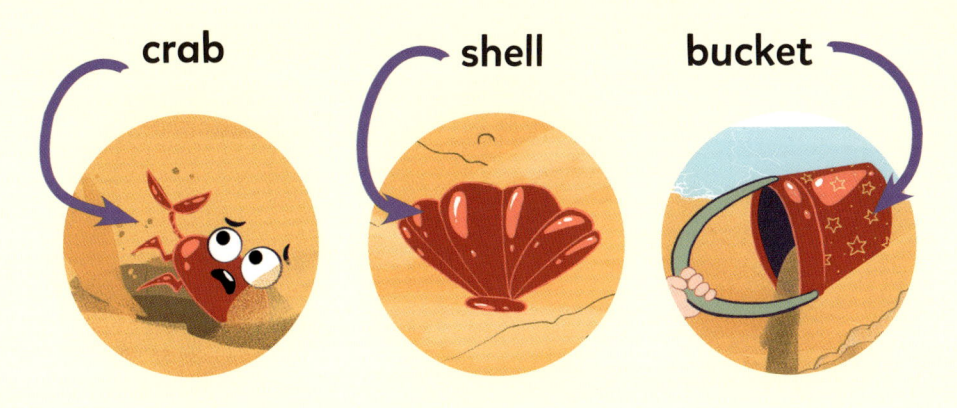

crab   shell   bucket

High-frequency words:
a she I it is the no we go his

Tips for Reading *Catch the Crab*

- Practice the words listed above before reading the story.
- If the reader struggles with any of the other words, ask them to look for sounds they know in the word. Encourage them to sound out the words and help them read the words if necessary.
- After reading the story, ask the reader how the crab got Dad's hat.

Fun Activity

Walk sideways like a crab!

Catch the Crab

Jess spots a crab.

"I must catch it!"

She digs and digs.

Is this the crab?

No, but it is a big rock.

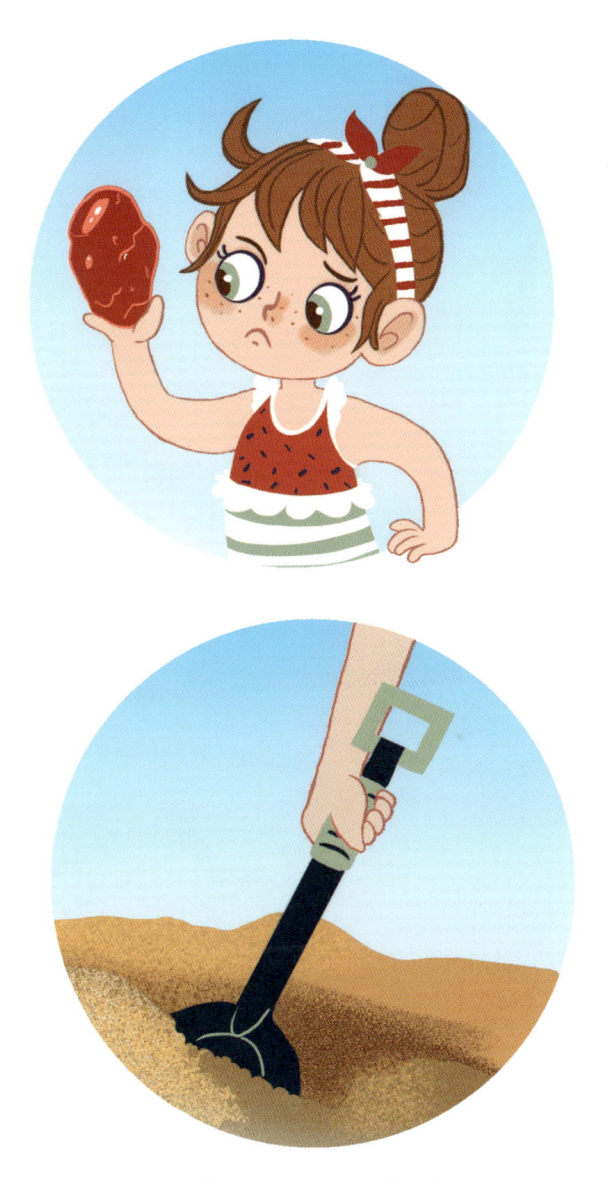

Jess digs and digs.

Is this the crab?

No, but it is a red shell.

Jess digs and digs.

Is this the crab?

No, but it is a fun bucket.

"We must go, Jess."

Dad looks for his hat.

He cannot spot it.

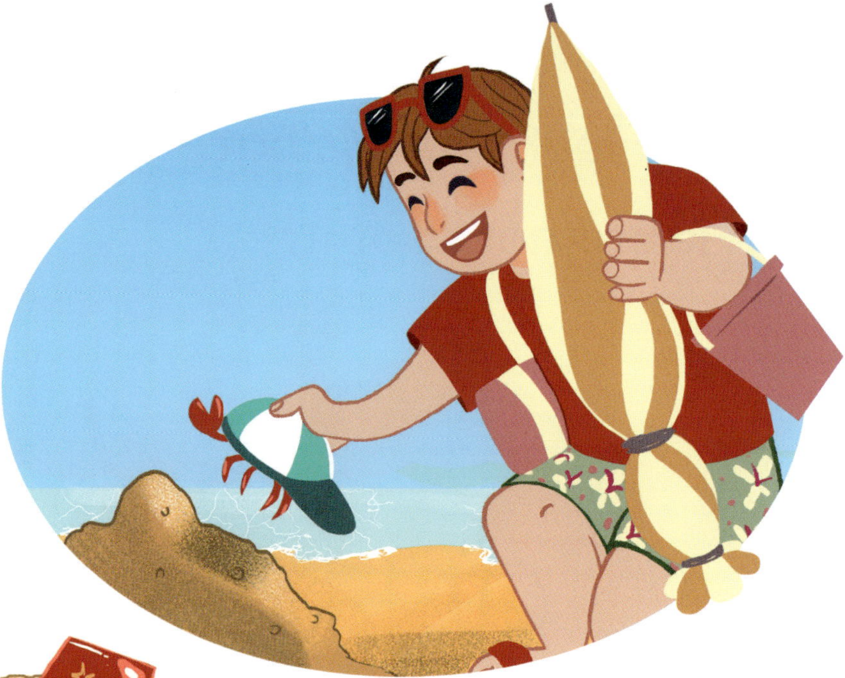

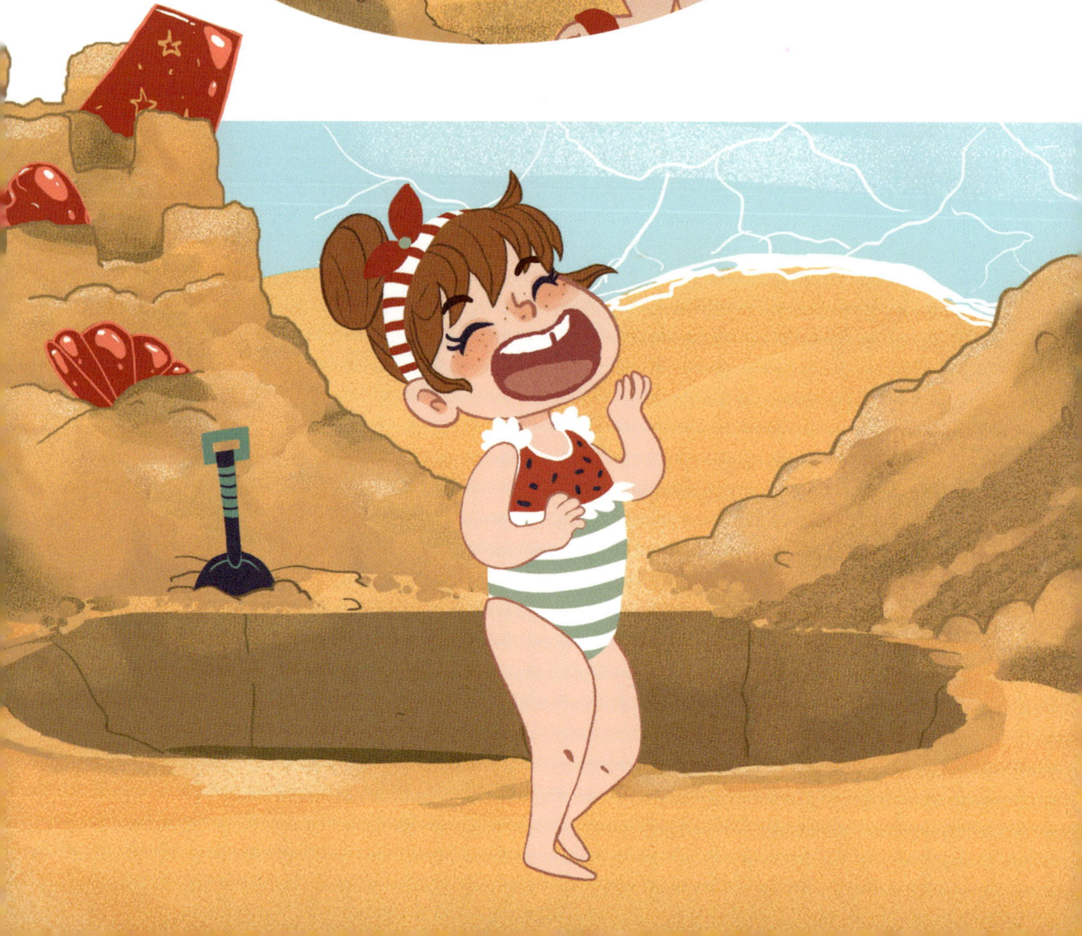

Look! Dad spots his hat . . .

. . . and the crab!

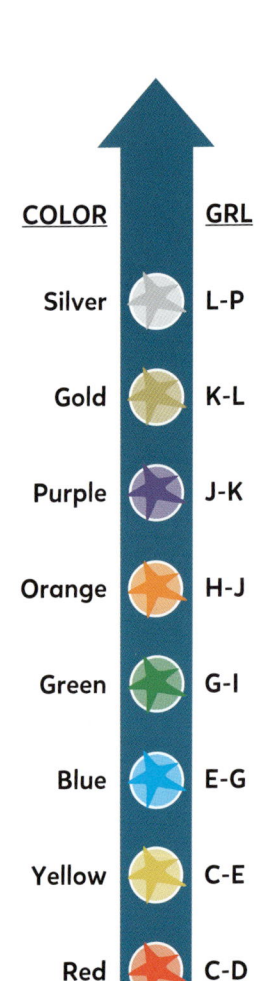

EARLY BIRD STORIES

Leveled for Guided Reading

COLOR	GRL
Silver	L-P
Gold	K-L
Purple	J-K
Orange	H-J
Green	G-I
Blue	E-G
Yellow	C-E
Red	C-D
Pink	A-C

Early Bird Stories have been edited and leveled by leading educational consultants to correspond with guided reading levels. The levels are assigned by taking into account the content, language style, layout, and phonics used in each book. Visit www.lernerbooks.com for more Early Bird Readers titles!

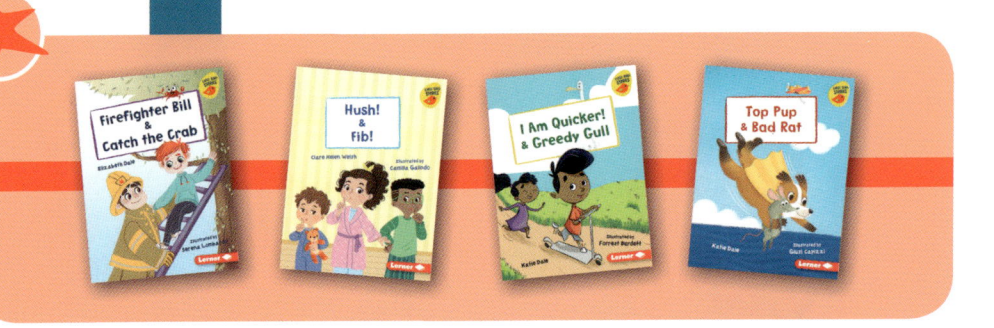